Chocolate Jungle

By Picasso Serge

Dedication

To my daughters, Tess and Jade

You are the light of my life and the heartbeat behind every word in this book. Your love, your strength, and your presence have shaped me in ways I could never fully express. This book is dedicated to you both, with all my love.

Acknowledgment

I would like to extend my deepest gratitude to my longtime girlfriend, Jade, whose unwavering support, patience, and encouragement carried me through every step of this publishing journey. Thank you for believing in me, standing by me, and giving me the strength to bring this book to life. I am truly grateful.

Two kids make a plan to get more treats from their unsuspecting dad, who is very busy snoozing in the backyard hammock.

Z z z

"Dad, could you tell us a story, please?" they asked.

Hank was used to telling stories to his kids. He actually enjoys telling stories to his kids more than working on his inventions. His latest invention is an invisible cloud catcher, but he's been trying to figure out why it doesn't work so well.

"Okay, kids, where would you like to go today?" he answers willingly. "But, I think today would be a good time for you to start helping me make up the story, okay?" he adds.

Whenever Hank tells one of his special stories, the threesome actually becomes part of the adventure. Oddly enough, it is only the kids who realize they can bring back souvenirs from the story.

"Can you tell us a story about a jungle made of chocolate?" asked little Kevin.

Kevin never gets tired of his dad's stories. Lately, though, he has grown an ENOURMOUS sweet tooth, his sister Becky says a mountain goat could get lost on that tooth. He doesn't mind, though, because he remembers what happened in the last story his dad told them. The story was about a fishing trip on the ocean. Kevin recalls how his sister's hand had turned into a hook, and before she could get her hand back, their dad had to tell a story about being attacked by a herd of boat–eating sea horses. That's a story for another time, though.

"Many years ago, kids in this neighborhood didn't have to ask for candy or treats from their mom or dad. That's because there once was a jungle made of pure milk chocolate right here in this backyard. We just had to go for a hike, and we found all the treats we could carry. If you look around, you might get lucky and find a smidgeon of melting brown treasure here somewhere, but of course you'd have to wrestle me for it if I found it first!" Hank says.

The Dad is so spellbound by the jungle story that he doesn't notice the kids have been busy eating chocolate like two monkeys in a banana shop. Kevin is having a blast because he hitches a ride on Dad's shoulders. He has no problem reaching all the thick chocolate vines hanging down. When he bites into a massive one, it squirts out creamy hot chocolate. Kevin is smiling from ear to ear and covered in chocolate from head to toe.

"Dad, are there any animals in this jungle?" Becky asked.

"Oh yes, all the animals you would normally see in a jungle can be found here, but here they're all made of chocolate."

"Are the insects made of chocolate, too?" Kevin asks.

"Yes, they are, but children listen, just like in a real jungle, you have to be very careful. Some especially wild insects want to keep kids from eating all this golden brown booty. They are known as Giant Butterwinkles. They are wrinkly butterflies with enormous wings," he says with alarm.

"They are friendly, but please be careful! If you see any Butterwinkles, run away as quickly as you can! These are not ordinary butterflies," the father continues.

"Are the wings as big as my Dragon kite?" Kevin asks.

"Bigger, and they also have very long, sticky legs that tickle the kids as they carry them out of the jungle. If they catch you, they will tickle you until you promise to share all your desserts with them for the rest of the day," he warns.

"Dad, look out, here comes one now," Kevin shouts.

"Kevin, let's escape down this marshmallow cliff while Dad distracts it," Becky says, keeping up with the storytelling.

Hank manages to outwit and outrun the pesky butterflies, but then finds himself all alone.

"Look out for the cliff, Dad!" shouts Becky.

Hank falls off the white soft cliff and tumbles forward end over end.

"He never was good at watching where he was going," laughs Becky.

"Oh look, he's going to fall right into the raging rainbow river of jellybeans!" Kevin says.

"Becky, do you think Dad can swim in jellybeans?" Kevin asks.

"I don't think he can," Becky replied, with a big smile.

"The river is flowing too fast, and I'm finding it difficult to stay above the jellybeans," Hank shouts out.

As their dad got closer, the kids realized what they
had to do.

Kevin and Becky managed to pull down some red
licorice vines that were growing near the river. As
Hank got closer, they threw him one end of the vine.
Luckily, red licorice was his favorite, so when he
caught it with his teeth, he just started eating the vine
to pull himself to safety.

"Thanks for throwing me a lifeline, kids. Tasted good, too. Well, have we had enough excitement for today?" Hank is starting to get a bit hungry from his afternoon nap.

"Oh yes, Dad! Thanks, it was awesome! Hope we can do it again soon," the kids replied, with big chocolaty grins on their faces.

"I see you've lost your sweet tooth, Kevin," Becky says.

"Your right. Mark another good tall tale from dad, and good job on your part too, Becky," Kevin says.

As all three got up to go inside, the kids watched as a mountain of chocolate chucks fell out of their dad's pockets.

The kids looked at each other and then grabbed as much as they could carry before running into the house, giggling because they knew something their dad didn't. Hank just stood there, wondering where all the candy had come from. He continued to have a puzzled look as he noticed his shoes were completely covered with chocolate. "Kids, do you know where all this candy came from?"

The End

9 781966 477532